D1558010

CARETTA
Caretta
A LOGGERHEAD TURTLE TALE

By **ELLEN GIORDANO**

Illustrated by **LIZ BEATTY**

Ellen Giordano

For Mimi, Essie, and Ange
and loving mothers everywhere.

The first thing I remember
is digging through the sand.
It was nighttime in the summer
this is how my life began.

At first, I felt confusion,
"Which direction should I head?"
But when I saw the moonlight,
I knew which way to tread.

I headed down the sandy dunes,
and scurried across the beach.
I knew if I was to survive,
the ocean I must reach.

When I tasted the salt water
And the waves carried me away,
I knew I had found my home,
a safe place for me to stay.

My flippers knew just what to do,
and swimming was such fun.
I dove into the deep blue sea,
my adventure had begun!

For years I swam through vast oceans,
Traveled thousands of miles of sea.
I gained over 300 pounds!
You would not have recognized me.

Then one day I felt a stirring,
a strong feeling in my heart.
It was time for me to return
to the place I got my start.

I swam for many miles
until my special beach I found
I pulled myself from the sea
and trudged across the ground.

My destiny was calling
so I worked throughout the night.
I dug a hole and laid my eggs,
I worked until first light.

At last, my work is over,
I'm headed back to sea,
I have a mother's wish
for turtles soon to be.

I hope my nest will be protected,
and my babies reach the sea,
So they can live a wonderful life
and fulfill their destiny.

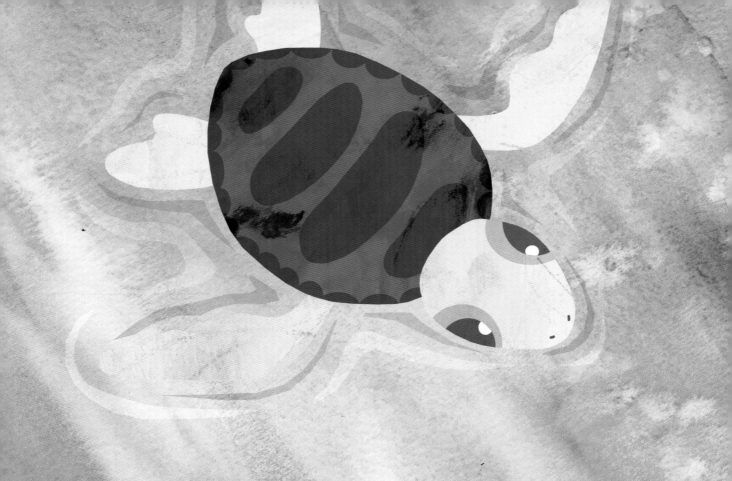

You can make a difference!
You play an important part,
To help baby turtles
get off to a great start.

Keep beach lights turned off,
so baby turtles can find the sea.
Remember to pick up all your trash,
so the beach is litter free.

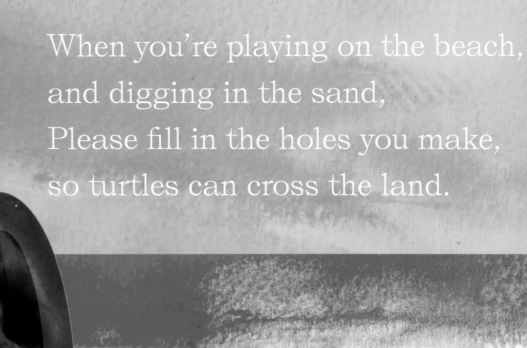

When you're playing on the beach,
and digging in the sand,
Please fill in the holes you make,
so turtles can cross the land.

It's time for me to say goodbye
and return to the ocean blue.
Thanks for listening to my tale
I loved sharing it with you.

Before you go, here are some loggerhead turtle facts you may like to know.

- 🐢 "Caretta caretta" is the scientific name for loggerhead turtles.

- 🐢 Loggerheads return to the beach where they were born to lay their eggs.

- 🐢 Loggerheads lay up to 100 eggs in their nest.

- 🐢 Loggerhead eggs take about 60 days to hatch.

- 🐢 New hatchlings are only two inches long.

- 🐢 Loggerheads grow to be three feet long and weigh over 300 pounds.

- 🐢 Loggerheads can live for over 50 years.

Caretta's Crew

As a part of Caretta's Crew,
I will help keep the beach safe for sea turtles.

_____

YOUR NAME